The Bad Trousers

The Bad Trousers

ROS ASQUITH

illustrations by Mairi Hedderwick

Barrington Stoke

First published in 2014 in Great Britain by
Barrington Stoke Ltd
18 Walker Street, Edinburgh, EH3 7LP

www.barringtonstoke.co.uk

The character of Robbie was created by Mairi Hedderwick for
Reading 2000 Storytime by Margaret Burnell, Sallie Harkness
and Helen McLullich (Oliver and Boyd/Longman Ltd, 1994).
Barrington Stoke gratefully acknowledges the origins of the
illustrations and the character of Robbie.

A CIP catalogue record for this book is available
from the British Library upon request

ISBN: 978-1-78112-428-4

Printed in China by Leo

This book has dyslexia friendly features

To Babette, with love – R.A.

For Robbie – M.H.

Contents

Chapter 1
Granny Knit

Robbie MacGregor lived in a tiny, windy, sunny village by the sea.

If you live in a big town, you may be surprised to know that there are whole villages, like Robbie's, that have just three shops, one school and one police station.

The police in Robbie's village spent most of their time playing tiddlywinks, because there were not many crimes to solve in the village. Robbie's mum said that this made the village a very charming place to live.

At one end of the village there was the Big House. It was so big that when Robbie was small he thought the king must live there. But there wasn't a king of the village and most people, like Robbie and his family, lived in cosy houses with stoves that burned peat. Peat, by the way, is a fuel – and not a funny spelling of Pete. It would not be charming to burn a person in the stove.

Robbie's family was his Granny Knit, his mum Effie, his dad Hector and a cat, Annie-Kit. Effie worked in the craft shop and Hector fished from dawn to dusk and then read the newspaper.

Robbie's granny was called Granny Knit because she liked to knit. She knitted egg cosies and hot water bottle covers and bed socks and blankets and pictures and even curtains.

But when Robbie told his friends about Granny Knit, they all guffawed and flapped like giggling sea lions until they fell over.

"Granny nit!" they squeaked.

"Does your granny have nits?" they yelled.

"Is your granny a nitwit?" they shouted.

Robbie turned pink, then red. "No, no, no!" he said. "Not that sort of nit. My granny knits scarves and jumpers and socks. And she sells them too, in the craft shop next to Mick's Stores."

"Oooh, will she knit me something?" Kirsty and Archie and Calum asked.

So Robbie stopped going pink and red.

But later that day, Robbie spoke to his mum. "I think we should call Granny Knit something else, because her name makes people laugh," he said.

"Oh, she's used to that." Robbie's mum smiled. "But now you're such a big boy, perhaps you had better call her by

her real name – Angusina Effie Mairead
Jean MacGregor."

Robbie decided to stick with Granny
Knit.

"Granny Knit's knitting is lovely," Robbie's mum said. "But I wish Granny Knit would keep out of the way when I'm cooking."

Robbie's mum was an amazing cook. But everything she liked to cook was very fancy. So Robbie often had rather odd dinners, like apricots with chilli, or fish with chocolate, or beef with bananas. And sometimes all Robbie wanted was a nice plate of beans on toast.

Robbie's mum's meals were one reason Robbie grew up to be a talented baker who baked only plain white bread and jam tarts. But that's another story.

Our story begins on a Thursday six weeks and one day before Robbie's birthday. Robbie is counting the days, and wondering what he will get.

I expect you are wondering why this story is called "The Bad Trousers". Perhaps you are also wondering how trousers can be naughty ...

Well, read on and you will discover.

Chapter 2
The Dream Tractor

Robbie and his mum were doing the weekly shop at Mick's Stores.

"My granny can knit everything. I think she could even knit the whole world," Robbie said to Mick.

"I bet she'll knit you something special for your birthday," Mick said.

"Oh no," Robbie said. "I don't want knitting. I want that red tractor."

Robbie had his eye on a fine red tractor you could sit on. It had a real steering wheel, and when you turned it the tractor wheels turned too. Robbie had been thinking about this tractor for nearly a year, since his last birthday. At his last birthday, his mum had said it was too big and cost too much – so instead he got a jigsaw puzzle with a picture of a tractor.

And now, in the shop, his mum shook her head again. "You need a new coat more than a tractor," she said.

Robbie put a brave face on it, and he picked out his favourite biscuits (jam ones with sprinkles).

"We need to get some cat food too," his mum said.

"Oh no, I don't think we do," said Robbie. "Annie-Kit is very fat."

"Oh Robbie, she isn't fat," his mum laughed.

"She is!" Robbie said. "She's as round as a muffin."

"She's round all right," his mum said, "but that's because she is having kittens."

"Kittens! Oh wow!" Robbie said. 'Maybe I'll get to keep a kitten for my birthday,' he thought.

But in his heart of hearts, Robbie thought he wasn't going to get kittens or the tractor. He'd get a new jacket, because his mum kept asking him about jackets.

"Do you like that one?" she asked.

"Not really," Robbie said, in the hope she would buy him the tractor.

anoraks

"What about this one?"

"No," Robbie said, with a bit less hope that she would still buy him the tractor.

"How about this one?"

"Not very much," Robbie said. "In fact, nothing is as nice as that red tractor with the excellent real steering wheel."

"A tractor won't keep you warm, will it?" his mum said. "You'd look pretty daft if you went round wearing a tractor. And you need a new bag for school. Your old one looks like a scarecrow's school bag."

"No it does not," Robbie said. "It's super smart. Anyway, scarecrows don't have bags."

"Yes they do," Mick interrupted. "They have secret bags full of birdseed and they bring them out at night, because they don't really like scaring birds."

"So that's why birds are never afraid of scarecrows," Robbie said. But he still hoped he wouldn't get a school bag for his birthday.

Chapter 3
Where Is Annie-Kit?

Robbie ran all the way home from Mick's Stores. He couldn't wait to see if Annie-Kit had had her kittens yet.

But Annie-Kit was nowhere to be found.

Was she in the garden?

Robbie peered under the wheelbarrow. He found 7 wood lice, 2 snails, 1 broken tea cup, and a mouse that scampered away like lightning.

But no Annie-Kit.

Then Robbie looked in the shed
where his dad kept old newspapers.
He found a washing line, 42 nails,
2 hammers, a chisel, 3 screwdrivers, a
rusty saw, 4 old bicycle wheels, 9 planks,
5 flower pots, a bucket and enough
string to tie up the world.

There was also a large cardboard box. It was taped together, so Annie-Kit couldn't be inside it. But there was a teeny hole. Robbie peered in. He could see a glimpse of something shiny and red. Could it be ... the tractor?

But Robbie was worried about Annie-Kit and so he made a bowl of her favourite food.

"Annie-Kit! Marvellous Mackerel!" Robbie called. "Kitty Chunks!" But still Annie-Kit didn't come.

'Perhaps she's in the washing basket,' he thought. But no, there was just a sock mountain in the washing basket, plus last year's jumper, which seemed to have shrunk.

"Dad," Robbie shouted. "We have to find Annie-Kit! She's missing!"

"Keep your shirt on," his dad said.
He sounded a bit absent-minded. "She's
probably just knitting up in her room."

"Dad! Not Granny Knit! It's
Annie-Kit! Annie-Kit is missing!" Robbie
shouted, and he tugged his dad's arm.
"What if she has her kittens? We have
to phone a vet ambulance!" he said.

"Calm down, Robbie," his dad said.
"Cats don't need vets to have their
babies. I think she's gone somewhere

private to have her kittens, and I think I know where that is. She'll have gone to the catmint patch – you know she loves the catmint."

"Come on, then," Robbie said, and he dragged his dad out to the catmint patch.

And sure enough, there was
Annie-Kit nestling in the catmint – with
her two little kittens. One was stripy,
and one was black and white like
Annie-Kit.

"Aha," Robbie's dad said. "So their father is that old pirate of a tom cat, Tiger."

"How do you know?" Robbie asked.

"Because old Tiger is as stripy as a zebra crossing." His dad laughed. "They are sweet. What a shame we can't keep them."

"Oh, but we can," Robbie said. "I'll look after them."

"You can have them until they're six weeks old," his dad said. "But then we've promised them to the postman, for his twins."

"But my birthday is in six weeks," Robbie said. "Please, please can I have the kittens?"

"You don't need mittens in the spring," his dad said.

But Robbie didn't think his dad's joke was funny. "Not mittens, kittens!"

Dad just ruffled Robbie's hair and yawned.

Chapter 4
Kitten Dreams

Robbie could not stop thinking about the kittens.

When he wasn't playing with them, he drew a picture of them for Granny Knit and a picture of them for his teacher.

He put the picture in his school bag
and showed it to the whole class.

"This one's called Zebra, and this one's called Rover," he said.

"Rover's not a cat's name – it's a dog's name!" said Calum.

"I'm going to train her so she can do tricks like a dog," Robbie said.

"But Rover is a boy dog's name! Not a girl's," said Archie.

"I don't care," said Robbie, and he didn't.

Robbie counted the days until his birthday.

41 ... 40 ... 39 ... 38 ...

Every night he dreamed of the tractor and the kittens. In some dreams,

Zebra and Rover were driving the tractor and in others Robbie was driving the tractor with the kittens sitting on his head. In one dream, the kittens were lost and he drove the tractor round the whole village and found them sheltering from the wind by the bus stop.

Every night Robbie begged to keep them.

"They like me so much," he said. "They'll be lonely without me."

"I think you mean you will be lonely without them," his dad said from behind his newspaper.

"But they'll miss you, too," Robbie said. "They think you're the best dad in the world."

"Nonsense," his dad said. "It's just cupboard love."

"Cupboard love? What's that?" Robbie asked.

"It means you love someone because they give you things," his dad said. "In this case, the cats love us because we gave them a nice warm basket and Granny Knit's balls of wool to play with."

Robbie thought for a minute or two.

"I'll still love you, even if you don't give me kittens. Or a tractor," he said.

Dad chuckled to himself. "Well, that's a relief," he said.

"But the kittens think you are the kind of dad who would want to give his son two kittens and a tractor for his birthday," Robbie said, with his sweetest smile. "And by the way, Dad, what's in that big box in the shed?"

"It's a flat pack unit to help with the cooking."

"What's flat pack?" Robbie asked.

"It's something you have to put together yourself," his dad told him.

Robbie was confused. "And how will it help with the cooking?" he asked.

"We can put the pots in a neat line and all the ingredients in order," his dad said. "Then perhaps your mum won't cook kippers with kiwi fruit or add sardines to the roast lamb."

"I heard that," Robbie's mum said. She was in the kitchen, tossing snails into a pot of strange green porridge. "I don't see any of you doing the cooking!"

"I'm out all day catching fish," Dad grumbled.

"And I'm in all day knitting," Granny Knit said.

"And I'm at school all day doing very hard things like writing and sums," said Robbie.

"Well, I do the washing and the ironing and the cleaning AND I work at the craft shop selling Granny Knit's knitting," his mum fumed.

The next day, the postman collected the kittens for his twins. Robbie cried as he waved goodbye to Rover and Zebra.

"My girls will be thrilled – one each," the postman said. "But I hope you get something special for your birthday tomorrow," he added, when he saw how sad Robbie was.

Robbie went to comfort Annie-Kit,

but she didn't seem to mind in the least.

Chapter 5
Robbie's Birthday

At last Robbie's birthday arrived.

"Happy birthday to me!
What fun it will be!
Happy birthday dear meeeeee!
Cake and biscuits for tea!"

When Robbie got home he saw Mum, Dad, Granny Knit and his favourite uncle – Uncle Poached Egg – all sitting on the sofa, waiting for him.

I'd love to tell you why Robbie's favourite uncle was called Uncle Poached Egg, but I'm afraid it's too long a story for this book.

Uncle Poached Egg told wonderful tales about how he'd sailed round the world and battled pirates and giant squid, all for the love of a beautiful woman. But Robbie had never met the beautiful woman, and now that he was a whole year older he had begun to

wonder if Uncle Poached Egg had ever
met her either.

Robbie took off his coat and hung
his school bag on the hook. He felt a bit
sad, because he could see his presents
were all on the small side. There wasn't
anything that looked like a tractor.

He got a new lunch box from Mum.

"Thank you for this very nice new lunch box. It will be excellent for, erm, putting my lunch in," Robbie said. "And it's much better than my old one, which was a bit stinky after you made those cod and crab buns last summer," he added. It was good to be honest.

His present from Dad was a pair of trainers.

"Thanks, Dad, for these great new trainers," Robbie said. "I'm sure they will help me run fast and ... They will be ... warmer than my old ones." Robbie couldn't think of anything more to say about the trainers – they were velcro and he wanted laces like Archie and Calum had.

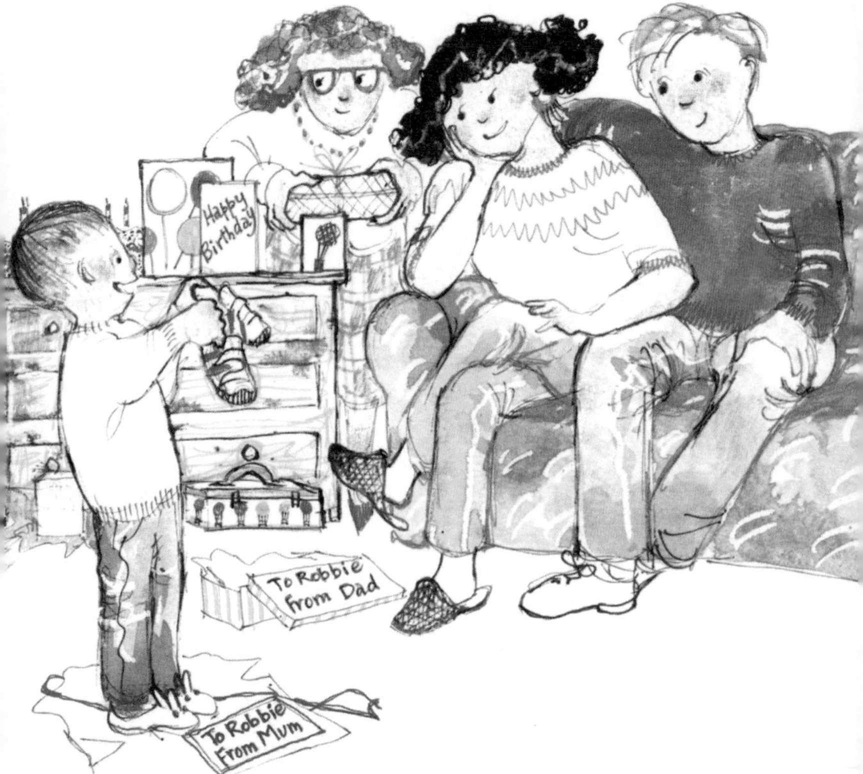
Happy Birthday
To Robbie from Dad
To Robbie From Mum

His present from Uncle Poached Egg was some coloured pencils.

"You can draw a picture of me battling a giant squid for the love of a beautiful mermaid," Uncle Poached Egg said.

"Thank you, Uncle Poached Egg," said Robbie. "But you never said she was a mermaid before."

It was Uncle Poached Egg's turn to turn pink, but Granny Knit saved him by choosing that moment to announce that she had a very special present for Robbie.

Robbie's eyes shone and his heart lifted. It must be the red tractor with the excellent real steering wheel that turned. At last!

But the parcel Granny Knit gave him did not look big enough to be the red tractor.

'Unless it's a flat pack tractor,' Robbie thought, with a little hope in his heart.

"Thank you, Angusina Effie Mairead Jean MacGregor," he said.

But as soon as Robbie took the package, he realised it was too soft to be a flat pack tractor. 'It's probably knitting,' he thought. Perhaps it was a new scarf. Or a jumper, because last year's jumper was now very small after it got shrunk in the wash.

But, oh no!

Chapter 6
The Trousers

Granny Knit's present was trousers.

Trousers!

Who in the whole of their life in the whole history of the world had ever, ever heard of knitted trousers?

Granny Knit saw the look on Robbie's face and misread it as joy. "I knew you'd like them," she said. "I made a lovely pattern of kittens, because you loved those kittens so much."

But Robbie's mum knew better.

"Come on," she whispered. "Put the trousers on to show Granny Knit and then we'll find a way to lose them."

So Robbie put on the horrible trousers, but he couldn't help his look of disgust as the itchy wool clung to his legs.

He felt like a baby. And he wanted to cry like a baby, too.

"He's had too much cake," his mum said.

"Now, there's just one more present," his dad said. "Silly me. I must have left it on the path when I got my keys out. Nip out and see if you can see it, Robbie."

Robbie was glad to get out of the room. He didn't want to cry and he didn't want to upset Granny Knit.

As he opened the front door, he hoped to see a shiny red tractor – but there, to his amazement, was a cat basket with both the kittens in it.

There was a note on the basket. It said –

"These kittens make us sneeze non-stop! And our dad told us how much you love them. So they are yours again. Happy birthday, Robbie! Love from the twins xxx."

"This is my best birthday ever,"
Robbie said. And he meant it.

When Robbie was tucked up asleep that night, Mum asked Granny Knit what she was going to knit now.

"I was going to knit a new fish blanket for Annie-Kit, because the kittens have stolen hers," Granny Knit said. "But do you know what Robbie said to me when I kissed him goodnight?"

"What was that?" Mum asked.

"He said, 'I love the kitty trousers so much that I'm going to give them to Annie-Kit to sleep on. That way, we'll always have them. Otherwise I'll grow out of them and we'll have to give them away.' Now, wasn't that sweet?" Granny Knit shook her head and chuckled.

Robbie's mum looked over and saw the kittens napping on the old fish blanket. Annie-Kit was snoozing on the Bad Trousers.

"Yes, Robbie's a good boy," said Mum, with a secret smile. "And do you know what? I'm saving up to buy him that red tractor for Christmas. I think he deserves it."

Chapter 7
Merry Christmas, Robbie!

So, now you know all about bad trousers.

Robbie did get his tractor for Christmas. And Granny Knit and Dad helped to cook a nice Christmas dinner – nothing too fancy. There was a big turkey with stuffing and sprouts and potatoes and gravy.

And then, when the last of the trifle was scraped from the bowl, everyone fell asleep on the sofa.

Except Robbie.

Robbie played all afternoon with Rover and Zebra and the excellent red tractor, giving the kittens rides all around the house.

Our books are tested
for children and young people by
children and young people.

Thanks to everyone who consulted on
a manuscript for their time and effort in
helping us to make our books better
for our readers.